First published 2011 by Nosy Crow Ltd
The Crow's Nest, 11 The Chandlery
50 Westminster Bridge Road
London SE1 7QY
www.nosycrow.com

ISBN 978 0 85763 004 9 (HB)

Nosy Crow and associated logos are trademarks and/or registered
trademarks of Nosy Crow Ltd

Text copyright © Nosy Crow 2011
Illustration copyright © Axel Scheffler 2011

The right of Axel Scheffler to be identified as the illustrator
of this work has been asserted.

A CIP catalogue record for this book is available from the British Library.

Printed in China

1 3 5 7 9 8 6 4 2

Pip and Posy

The Little Puddle

Axel Scheffler

nosy crow

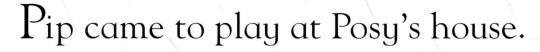

Pip came to play at Posy's house.

He hung up his coat and took off his wellies.

"What shall we play?"
said Posy.

First, they decided to take
their babies for a walk.

Next, they built a big train track and a town.

Then they stopped for a snack.

Pip was **very** thirsty!

After that, Pip and Posy
pretended to be lions.

And they had such fun **roaring** that
Pip forgot he needed a wee.

Suddenly, there was
a little puddle
on the floor.

Oh dear!

"Never mind, Pip,"
said Posy.

"Everyone has accidents sometimes."

Posy gave Pip some of her clothes to wear.

They spent the rest of the day painting pictures.

And the next time Pip had to have a wee,
he did it in the potty.

All by himself.

Then it was time for a bath.
With lots of bubbles.

Hooray!